I WISH TONIGHT
Copyright © 2000 by Good Books, Intercourse, PA 17534
International Standard Book Number: 1-56148-315-X
Library of Congress Catalog Card Number: 00-030843

Library of Congress Cataloging-in-Publication Data

Rock, Lois
  I wish tonight / Lois Rock ; illustrated by Anne Wilson.
    p. cm.
  Summary: A child wishes for a world of goodness, laughter, and
fun and receives his wish in a dream.
  ISBN 1-56148-315-X
  [1. Wishes--Fiction. 2. Dreams--Fiction. 3. Stories in rhyme.]
I. Wilson, Anne (Anne Catherine), 1974-ill. II. Title.

PZ8.3.R58615 Iw 2000
[E]--dc21   00-030843

I Wish Tonight

Lois Rock Illustrated by Anne Wilson

Good Books
Intercourse, PA 17534
800/762-7171

The evening sky darkens, the stars will shine bright,
But which is the first star that I'll see tonight?
I wish that I may, oh, I wish that I might
Have everything that I wish for tonight.

I wish for a silver moon sailing on high

Through the shape-shifting oceans of clouds in the sky

And a warm gentle breeze that will sing and will sigh

In the tall swaying treetops as it passes by.

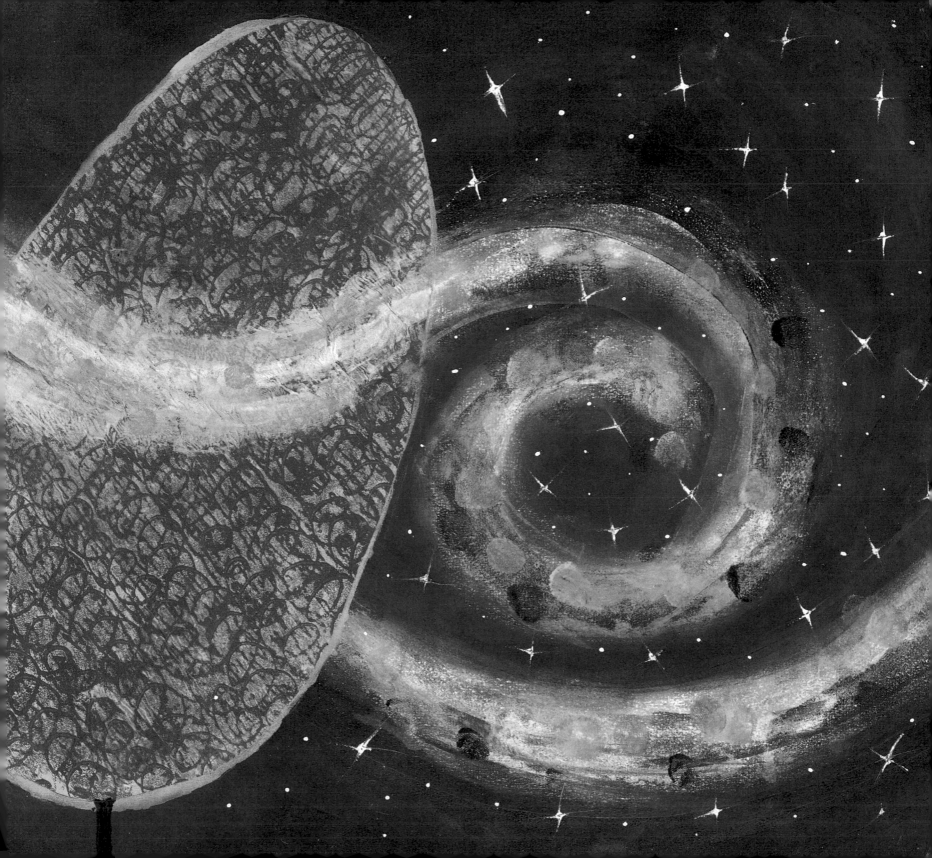

I wish for a bed with a sail and an oar

That will float on the shadows so dark on the floor;

As the wind fills the sails to the sky it will soar

And take me up high to a faraway shore.

In the land of beyond all my dreams will come true.

I'll do all the things that I so want to do;

I'll have great adventures the whole long day through...

So I'll wish for my friends to be there with me too.

All the things that we need will be ours just for free
With enough for my friends—oh, and their friends—and me,
We'll pick what we want just like fruit from a tree;
Everyone in the world will come nearer to see.

We'll tell them that nothing can be bought or sold:
In the land that I wish for no one will need gold.
We'll pick lovely presents for young and for old
So no one goes hungry, and no one is cold.

Then one to another we'll say, 'Let's be friends,
And let's make a great plan: that together we'll mend
Anything that is broken, and carefully tend
Everything in the world; keep it safe to the end.'

Soon, no one will know where the wastelands have been:
The trees will grow tall and the deserts turn green,
The air will blow clear and the rain will fall clean,
And in shimmering streams silver fish will be seen.

The animals then will draw close without fear—
The shy little shrew will be first to come near,
Then musk ox, okapi, wapiti and deer.
Imagine the squeaking, the grunting, the cheer!

Then I'll call for quiet: 'Hush, everyone, please,
Let's listen to songbirds high up in the trees,
And after they've finished, the soft sighing breeze,
The rippling brooks, and the tumbling seas.'

I'll go down to the shore in the gold evening light

And climb back on my boat, sail off in the night,

While the skies turn to dark and the stars shine so bright

And I'll wish for a world where what's wrong is put right.

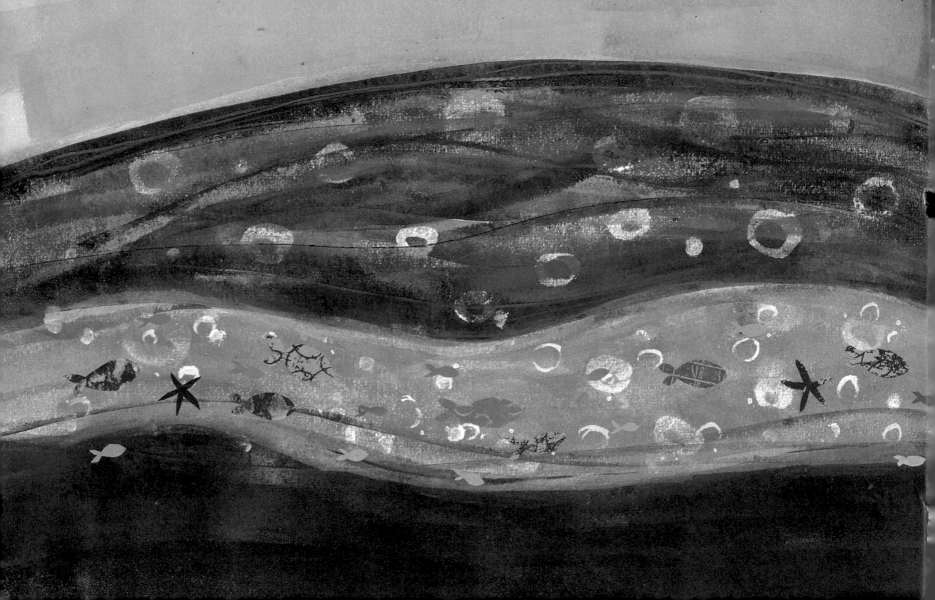

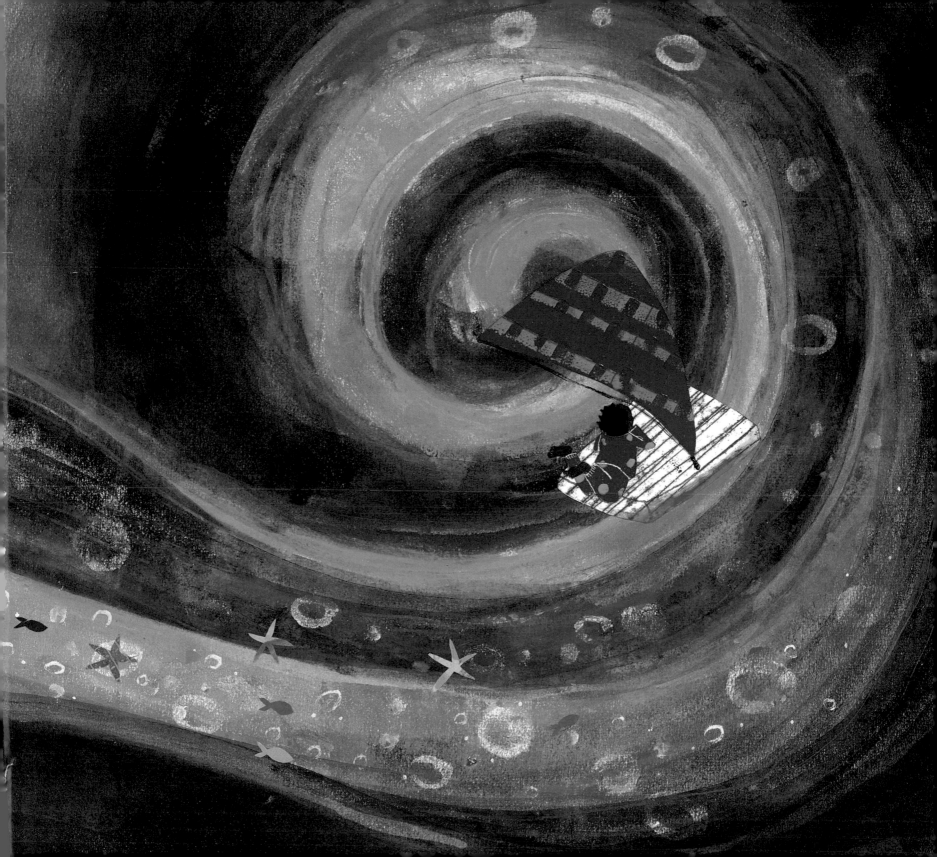

And then, in the morning, I'll wake with the sun,
My dream won't be over, my dream's just begun:
A dream full of goodness and laughter and fun
For me, for the world, and for everyone.